You Choose Stories: Justice League
is published by Stone Arch Books,
A Capstone Imprint
1710 Roe Crest Drive
North Mankato, Minnesota 56003
www.mycapstone.com

STAR40191

Cataloging-in-Publication Data is available
on the Library of Congress website.
ISBN: 978-1-4965-6555-6 (library binding)
ISBN: 978-1-4965-6559-4 (paperback)
ISBN: 978-1-4965-6563-1 (eBook)

Summary: The sorceress Circe has turned
Justice League men into Beastiamorph servants,
and now she's ready to take over a faraway
planet! With your help, can Wonder Woman,
Supergirl, Zatanna, and other Justice League
heroes prevent Circe's *Cosmic Conquest*?

Printed in Canada.
PA020

DC SUPER HEROES

← YOU CHOOSE →

JUSTICE LEAGUE

COSMIC CONQUEST

written by
Laurie S. Sutton

illustrated by
Erik Doescher

Fountaindale Public Library
Bolingbrook, IL
(630) 759-2102

STONE ARCH BOOKS
a capstone imprint

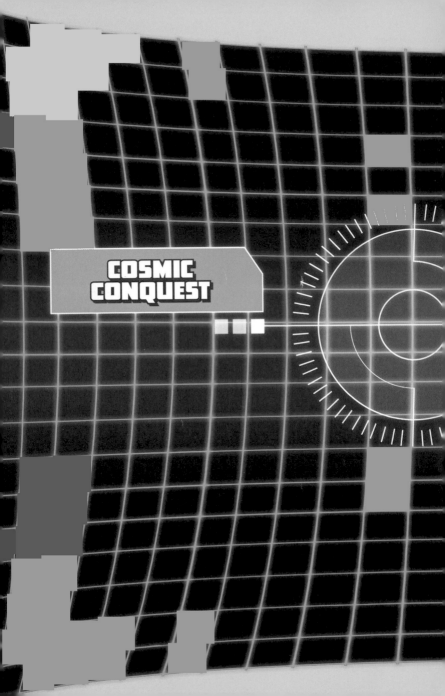

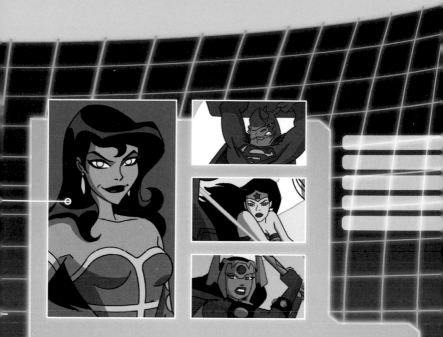

The sorceress Circe has turned Justice League men into Beastiamorph servants, and now she's ready to take over a faraway planet! With your help, can Wonder Woman, Supergirl, Zatanna, and other female Justice League heroes prevent Circe's *Cosmic Conquest*?

Follow the directions at the bottom of each page. The choices YOU make will change the outcome of the story. After you finish one path, go back and read the others for more Justice League adventures!

The Watchtower circles high above Earth. This giant space station is the headquarters of the Justice League, the World's Greatest Super Heroes. Today many of the members have come aboard for a meeting.

The Flash squirms in his seat. He doesn't like staying still. Nearby, Green Arrow shows Cyborg and Huntress his latest trick arrows while Aquaman talks with Power Girl and Black Canary. Zatanna entertains Big Barda and Supergirl with a few card tricks.

When Superman, Batman, and Wonder Woman enter the room, all the members settle. "OK," the Man of Steel says. "Let's bring this meeting to order—"

WAHBOOM!

A burst of light suddenly explodes in the middle of the gathering. When it fades, a woman with purple hair and a bright green outfit stands on top of the meeting table.

"Circe!" Wonder Woman exclaims.

Turn the page.

The villain grins. "Oops, am I interrupting something? Sorry. I just came to grab a few things," Circe says.

"Stop her!" Zatanna shouts.

The Justice League members leap into action. They know this intruder. She's Circe, the sorceress of ancient myth. Her magical powers are legendary.

The half man, half machine super hero Cyborg shoots a blast from his sonic arm cannon. Black Canary adds her ear-splitting Canary Cry. Superman flies over with his heat-vision ablaze.

But Circe doesn't run. She simply raises her hand, and a wave of magic ripples outward.

Suddenly the male super heroes start to transform. Their human heads and limbs shift and grow. Scales, feathers, and horns appear.

"Circe is turning them into animals!" Zatanna shouts.

"Not just animals—Beastiamorphs," Wonder Woman says. "They're becoming her slaves."

"*Lleps s'ecriC pots!*" Zatanna shouts. She speaks backward to cast her own spell.

But it's not strong enough to stop Circe's magic. The men turn into beasts as the women watch. Cyborg looks like a bear! Aquaman becomes part shark!

"You can't stop me," Circe says. "I plan to conquer worlds beyond this planet. I've already picked one. It only has three empires to crush, and the Justice League is going to help me do it!"

Circe wraps her magical energy around the Beastiamorph super heroes. Then she teleports off the Watchtower, taking them with her. **POOF!**

"Where did she go?" Huntress asks.

"*EcriC em wohs,*" Zatanna says, casting another spell.

A glowing sphere forms in the air. Like a crystal ball, it shows Circe in a place covered with mountains.

"She only has two Beastiamorphs with her," Big Barda says. "Where are the others?"

Turn the page.

Zatanna widens the spell. It reveals the location of the rest of their transformed friends. Beastiamorphs Aquaman and Batman are attacking innocent villagers. Green Arrow and The Flash are battling warriors on horseback.

"We need to protect the people on that planet and make Circe return our friends to human form," Black Canary says. "Zatanna, can you teleport us there with one of your spells?"

"Yes," Zatanna replies.

"Good. We'll split into three teams," Wonder Woman says. "Barda, you and I have the strength to take on Superman and Cyborg. Huntress and Power Girl have the skills to face Batman and Aquaman. Black Canary, Zatanna, and Supergirl can tackle Green Arrow and The Flash."

"I'll transport you all there and catch up later," Zatanna says. Before her friends can ask why she's staying behind, Zatanna speaks her backward spell. *"Tenalp eht ot nemow eht tropsnart!"*

POOF! The super heroes disappear.

As soon as her friends are gone, Zatanna speaks another backward spell.

"*Raeppa, nagirtE!*" Zatanna says.

POOF! The demon Etrigan appears. Even though he looks like a monster, Etrigan is a hero and a member of the Justice League.

"Etrigan, I need your help fighting Circe," Zatanna says. "She's turned male Justice League members into Beastiamorphs."

The demon frowns. "Circe is up to her old tricks. But because I am not human, her transformation spell cannot affect me," he replies.

"Exactly. You also have powerful abilities. If we combine our magical skills, we have a chance to defeat Circe and save our friends," Zatanna says. "And since you weren't here when Circe attacked, she won't be expecting you. We'll have the element of surprise."

Etrigan grins. "I love surprises. Now let's get going."

To follow Wonder Woman and Big Barda, turn to page 12.
To follow Power Girl and Huntress, turn to page 14.
To follow Black Canary and Supergirl, turn to page 16.

Wonder Woman and Big Barda are teleported to the faraway planet by Zatanna. They arrive to see the Superman and Cyborg Beastiamorphs attacking a mountaintop fortress. Superman still wears his uniform, but his head and limbs look like a rhinoceros. Cyborg is now half machine, half bear!

THUNK! THUNK!

Superman rams the walls of the fortress. Giant stone blocks tumble to the ground.

BLAAAM!

Cyborg shoots his sonic arm cannon at warriors protecting the fortress. The people look human, except they have bright blue skin.

Circe hovers in the air and hurls magical energy down at the warriors. Their simple iron swords and armor are useless against her attack.

"Defeating the Mountain Kingdom is the first step to conquering this world!" Circe declares. "Once the other two empires fall, the planet will be mine."

Big Barda looks out at the raging battle. "Those people are no match for Circe and two Beastiamorphs," she says.

"But we are," Wonder Woman replies. "With our super-strength, we can take Circe down."

The two take a mighty leap toward Circe in a double-team attack. But Circe is busy enjoying all the destruction. She doesn't even realize Wonder Woman and Barda are on the planet—until they slam into her.

WHAAAAM!

The impact sends Circe flying beyond a nearby mountaintop.

"Arrrgh! How did they know where to find me?" she screams. She quickly teleports back to the fortress. She's full of fury.

"Beastiamorphs, attack the heroes!" Circe orders. Then she sends a rain of magical fire down on the native warriors.

The heroes must decide whom to fight first.

If Wonder Woman and Barda fight Circe, turn to page 18.
If they battle the Beastiamorphs, turn to page 25.

Huntress and Power Girl arrive on the planet. Zatanna's spell has placed them in the middle of a village. The two are surrounded by homes with gardens. They stand on a street paved with crushed seashells. But the town seems deserted.

"Where is everyone?" Huntress wonders.

CRASSSSH! BLAAAM! WHOOMP!

"That sounds like a battle!" Power Girl says.

Huntress takes out her crossbow to get ready. She doesn't have Power Girl's super-strength, but she does have superior fighting skills.

Power Girl lifts Huntress with her as she flies into the sky. That's when they see two Beastiamorphs fighting blue-skinned townspeople at the base of a nearby tower. They also see that they're not above an ordinary village. Even though the ground and houses look normal, they're on the deck of a gigantic ship sailing on a huge ocean.

"It's a floating town," Power Girl realizes. Then she points toward similar vessels sailing together. "It's a *fleet* of floating town ships."

"This must be one of the empires Circe wants to conquer," Huntress says.

"The people don't stand a chance against the Beastiamorphs. Look! It's Aquaman and Batman," Power Girl exclaims.

Aquaman has the head of a shark and a dorsal fin on his back. Batman has the features of a bat, including giant leathery wings.

"The villagers are defending that tower. It must be important," Power Girl says. "Maybe it's the fleet's command center."

"So whoever controls the tower controls the whole fleet," Huntress adds. "That must be Circe's plan. We have to stop her."

Power Girl flies toward the tower with Huntress under her arm. Suddenly a burst of magical energy knocks them to the deck. Circe has teleported into the battle!

"Look who's joined the party," Power Girl says to Huntress. "Do you want to say 'hello' or should I?"

If Power Girl attacks Circe, turn to page 20.
If Huntress makes the first move, turn to page 27.

Zatanna's teleportation spell lands Black Canary and Supergirl in the middle of a raging battle! Blue-skinned warriors on horseback charge toward them from opposite directions. The warriors wear leather helmets and armor made from thick, quilted cloth. They carry spears and bows and arrows.

"Get us into the air!" Black Canary says. Supergirl grabs her teammate and launches away.

From the sky, the super heroes get a clear view of the battle. The horse riders weren't attacking Black Canary or Supergirl. They aren't attacking each other, either. They're all heading toward a tornado that's threatening a large group of wagons. Supergirl uses her super-vision to get a closer look.

"That's The Flash. He's been turned into a cheetah beast!" Supergirl exclaims. "He's running in circles at super-speed to create a tornado. And he's using it to attack all those wagons. They must be the warriors' homes."

"This must be one of the empires Circe wants to conquer. It's like the traveling Mongol and Hun tribes on ancient Earth," Black Canary says.

SCREEEE!

A loud screech splits the air. But it isn't Black Canary's powerful voice. It's Beastiamorph Green Arrow! Huge wings on his back push him through the sky. He has the head of a hawk but still has human-like hands to fire arrows at the warriors below.

"Maybe we should've brought Hawkgirl along," Canary says.

"Oh, don't worry. I can take care of these guys," Supergirl says confidently.

Suddenly the ground rumbles. Gigantic arms made of dirt burst up from the earth and knock down the warriors on horseback.

"That's Circe's sorcery! She's a bigger threat than the Beastiamorphs right now. We have to deal with her first. But how?" Canary asks.

If Supergirl goes after Circe alone, turn to page 23.
If the teammates attack together, turn to page 29.

Wonder Woman and Big Barda decide Circe is the biggest threat. If they defeat her, they can make her reverse the Beastiamorph spell.

"Your road to cosmic conquest is a dead end, Circe!" Wonder Woman shouts. She leaps out of the way of the Beastiamorphs and right at the villain.

"You Amazons have always been such a pain," Circe replies.

The sorceress creates a huge ball of magical energy. It shoots bolts of lightning at Wonder Woman. But the Amazon Princess raises her bracelets and crosses them in front of her face.

BWOOOOM!

The energy bounces off the bracelets.

"I guess you've never met a warrior from the planet Apokolips," Barda tells Circe as she energizes her Mega-Rod weapon. "I will show you real pain!"

Big Barda powers up the flight discs on her boots. She zooms into the air and strikes Circe with the Mega-Rod.

KABLAAAM!

The hit sends Circe spinning, but she quickly flies back. "Now you've made me mad," she says.

"Bring it on," Barda replies.

The two super heroes face the sorceress. Barda tightens her grip on the crackling Mega-Rod. Wonder Woman reaches for her golden lasso. The teammates move toward Circe.

"Hmph! I don't have time for you two. I have other empires to conquer," Circe says and then teleports away. **POOF!**

"Coward," Barda mumbles.

"I agree. But now we have other problems," Wonder Woman says.

Transformed Superman and Cyborg have been busy. They've gone back to smashing and blasting the warriors defending the mountain fortress.

"We have no choice. We have to fight our friends," Wonder Woman says.

If Wonder Woman and Barda split up and each take on a Beastiamorph, turn to page 32.

If they work together, turn to page 49.

"I'll take care of this magical menace,"
Power Girl says.

She quickly sets Huntress down in the village.
Then she launches at Circe with super-speed.
But just before Power Girl makes impact,
Circe teleports away. **POOF!**

Power Girl rockets through the empty air.
She's going so fast she can't stop. Her speed
carries her beyond the town ship and out to sea.

POOF! Circe reappears in front of a group
of houses. She glares at Huntress. "How did the
League find me?" she exclaims. "No matter.
I won't let you stand in my way."

She sends out a wave of magical energy.
The buildings around her suddenly sprout
mechanical legs! They rise up and stomp toward
Huntress. A family inside one of the houses
shouts from the window for help.

Huntress runs toward the house to rescue the
people. But Circe isn't about to make it easy.

BZAAAP! BZOWWW!

Turn to page 22.

Circe lifts into the air and fires bolts of magic. Huntress runs between the houses' legs to dodge the blasts.

BLAAAM!

A bolt destroys a leg on the family's home. The house starts to fall over!

"Oops!" Circe laughs. She flies off toward the central tower.

"Yaaaa!" the people inside yell.

"I've got it," Power Girl says, zooming over.

She swoops under the house. With her super-strength, she stops it from smashing into the deck. The other, empty houses stagger around.

Once the home is safely on the ground, the family rushes out. They raise their spears and run toward the central tower to join the fight against the Beastiamorphs.

"We must help the villagers protect that tower from Circe," Huntress tells Power Girl. "And I know how to do it."

If Huntress tries a risky plan, turn to page 34.
If Huntress says to split up, turn to page 52.

"I can handle Circe," Supergirl says.

She puts Black Canary on the ground. Then she flies toward the thrashing arms made out of dirt and magic.

"Hey! Don't you leave me out of the action!" Canary shouts. But it seems that Supergirl's super-hearing is "turned off" at that moment.

Supergirl sees Circe standing in the center of the mud limbs. The sorceress waves her arms, and the magical arms follow her movements. She swipes at the horse riders, and they are smacked down.

Supergirl zooms at Circe in a blur of super-speed and delivers a mighty punch.

POWWW!

Circe is soaring through the air before she even realizes the hero arrived.

Supergirl shrugs. "She's not so tough."

Then she sees Circe transform into something unbelievable.

Turn the page.

The sorceress' arms turn into wings, and her feet become talons. Her torso grows feathers. She's a Harpy from Greek myth!

The half woman, half bird monster charges at Supergirl. The hero zips away like a sparrow. With her super-speed, Supergirl knows she can fly circles around the sorceress.

But then Circe-Harpy claps her wings together, and a wave of magical energy surges at Supergirl. It knocks her out of the sky. She hits the ground, stunned. Circe-Harpy swoops toward her victim.

EEEEEEE! A sonic scream hits Circe-Harpy and knocks her back from Supergirl and across the meadow.

"Stay away from my friend!" Black Canary declares as she gallops over on a warhorse.

The sorceress races back to return the attack. Black Canary must decide how to defeat this monster threat.

If Black Canary tricks Circe, turn to page 36.

If Black Canary blasts the sorceress with a Canary Cry, turn to page 55.

The transformed Justice League men start charging toward their teammates. It's suddenly very obvious which foe Wonder Woman and Big Barda need to fight first!

Cyborg shoots an energy blast from his fist cannon at Wonder Woman. She holds up her bracelets like a shield, and the blast bounces back at him.

BWHAAAM!

The impact sends Beastiamorph Cyborg crashing into the fortress wall. He drops to the ground and does not get up.

"I guess he can dish it out, but he can't take it," Wonder Woman says.

Nearby, Superman flies at Barda faster than a speeding bullet. She stands her ground like a batter in a baseball game and hits the Beastiamorph with her Mega-Rod.

POW!

He goes flying backward through the air.

"Home run," Barda says.

Turn the page.

With the Beastiamorphs taken care of, Wonder Woman and Big Barda turn to their other foe. They leap into the air to battle Circe.

KZAAAT! KZAAAT!

The sorceress blasts bolts of magic from above. Barda returns fire with her Mega-Rod.

BLAAA-WHOOOM!

The two energies crash into each other and erupt in a huge explosion. The blast throws the heroes against the fortress wall. When they get back to their feet, Circe is gone.

"I can find her with my Mother Box," Barda says. She pulls a small cube from her belt. "It's tech from my planet. It has many functions."

But the trouble at the fortress isn't over. The Beastiamorphs are getting back to their feet too.

"I'll stay here and protect the warriors," Wonder Woman says. "Go after Circe!"

Big Barda hesitates. Can she leave her teammate to fight alone?

If Barda teleports after Circe, turn to page 68.
If Barda stays to fight the Beastiamorphs, turn to page 87.

With lightning reflexes, Huntress readies her crossbow. She sends bolts flying at Circe.

The sorceress swoops out of the way, but it's just enough of a distraction. Power Girl zooms over and punches her foe right in the stomach.

Circe smacks into the ground. "The Justice League! Can't a sorceress conquer a planet without interference?" she groans. She's so angry that she casts the first spell that comes to mind.

The villain starts to transform. Her arms turn into clacking claws. Her body forms a hard, crab-like shell with spikes. She sprouts eight legs and a long, serpent neck with a viper head.

"Ugh!" Huntress grimaces at the sight.

The Circe monster swipes a huge claw at Huntress, but Power Girl rushes in. She blocks the blow with her invulnerable body. The impact knocks her out to sea. Circe raises her claw once more to crush the other hero.

Huntress stands her ground and aims her mini crossbow at the giant monster. Circe hisses with laughter.

Turn the page.

Suddenly Power Girl bursts out of the water, covered in seaweed. She shakes off the plants and speeds toward the Circe monster.

The villain is so focused on Huntress she doesn't see Power Girl coming.

KA-POWWW!

Power Girl delivers another super-punch.

Circe slides across the deck, taking out homes and gardens as she goes. She smashes a path through the village and almost falls overboard. Circe saves herself by using her claws to hang onto the side.

But the monster's extreme weight tips the ship. The deck tilts, and everyone on it starts to tumble toward the Circe monster—including Huntress, the Beastiamorphs, and the villagers. Power Girl hovers in midair and watches this new danger unfold.

"I have to make Circe let go of the ship, but how?" Power Girl wonders.

If Power Girl stomps on the monster, turn to page 72.
If Power Girl uses her heat-vision, turn to page 89.

Supergirl knows they're stronger together. She and Black Canary fly over to the sorceress.

Circe stands in the center of a circle of giant hands that stretch up from the ground. They're made of dirt and grass, and they sway like cobras. Circe makes a sweeping gesture, and the hands swipe at the horse riders. Then she sees Supergirl and Black Canary hovering in the sky above.

"The Justice League! I'm not going to let you spoil my fun," Circe growls. She sends the hands up to grab the super heroes.

"You have a lousy idea of fun," Supergirl says. She flies higher and out of reach.

The hands keep stretching up and up. Supergirl blows a gust of icy super-breath at the hands, and they freeze solid. Then Black Canary unleashes a shrill Canary Cry.

EEEEEEEEE!

The giant hands shatter. Chunks of frozen dirt slam into the ground around Circe.

BWHAAAM! BWHAAAM!

Turn the page.

Circe holds her arms over her head to protect against the falling boulders. The rest of the dirt hands do the same.

Supergirl blasts her heat-vision at the villain. Circe returns fire with a flurry of magical bolts. Supergirl avoids them with super-speed, but one hits Black Canary and knocks her out.

The sorceress laughs in triumph. "One down, one to go," she says. "Then this planet is mine."

POOF! Suddenly Zatanna and Etrigan appear in a puff of colorful smoke.

"I like that teleportation spell. It tickles," Etrigan says with a chuckle.

"More Justice League?" Circe shouts.

Etrigan immediately hurls a stream of demon fire at Circe. Soon a great ball of fire surrounds her. The sphere shakes as Circe tries to escape the flaming prison.

Zatanna watches the ball of fire and wonders if she should help Etrigan.

If Zatanna lets Etrigan handle Circe, turn to page 74.
If Zatanna helps her teammate, turn to page 93.

"Let's split up," Wonder Woman tells Barda. "I'll deal with Superman."

As Big Barda takes off to face Cyborg, Wonder Woman wonders just how she's going to battle her teammate.

"First, I have to stop him from attacking the fortress. Hmm. I have an idea for a distraction," Wonder Woman says.

She picks up a stone block from the destroyed fortress wall. Then she hurls it at the Beastiamorph.

WHAAAAM!

The stone shatters against Superman's rhinoceros back. But he hardly notices. He keeps ramming the wall.

"Maybe I need a bigger distraction," Wonder Woman says.

Using her amazing Amazon strength, she lifts a huge stone statue. She swings it like a baseball bat at Superman.

POWWWW!

The statue breaks in two, but it gets the Beastiamorph's attention. He turns away from the fortress wall and glares at Wonder Woman.

"*That* worked," she says.

ZZZZZT!

Twin beams of heat-vision blaze from Superman's rhino eyes. Wonder Woman holds up her bracelets. The beams bounce off the polished metal and straight back at Superman.

"Yaaargh!" Superman howls as the heat-vision blasts into his animal skin.

The Amazon Princess leaps over and smacks her bracelets against the sides of Superman's rhino-like head. He staggers. Then he lifts off the ground, trying to escape.

"Not so fast!" Wonder Woman says.

She grabs her golden lasso and twirls it above her head. She tosses it at Superman and catches him like a bull at a rodeo. Wonder Woman is pulled into the air behind the Beastiamorph.

Turn to page 38.

"I have a plan to stop Circe, but it's risky. It all depends on how tough she is," Huntress says. She explains her idea to Power Girl.

"That sounds like a scene from an old movie I saw once," Power Girl replies. "It's worth a try."

Power Girl puts an arm around Huntress and flies into the air. They hover above the central tower.

Circe and the Beastiamorphs are battling the villagers. Aquaman snaps his huge shark-like jaws at their simple spears. Batman sweeps them aside with his giant, leathery wings. Circe hurls bolts of magical energy.

"OK, here goes phase one," Huntress says. She drops into the middle of the fight below.

Huntress lands in front of Circe and aims her mini crossbow at the sorceress. Circe looks at Huntress and the crossbow, and she laughs.

"Is that supposed to scare me?" Circe says.

Circe launches a burst of magical energy at Huntress. The hero dodges the attack using her acrobatic skills and fires a crossbow bolt at the sorceress. Circe transforms it into a snake in midair. It falls to the ground and slithers away.

Huntress turns and runs.

"You super heroes aren't so brave after all," Circe says. She fires another round of energy at Huntress' back.

But Huntress leaps out of the way just in time. The crackling energy hits Aquaman instead.

"Rhaaargh!" the Beastiamorph howls. He blindly strikes out with his trident and accidentally whacks Circe.

The sorceress is knocked backward through the crowd of the battling villagers. She finally stops when she hits a large boulder with a **THUNK!**

Circe stands back up. Her eyes blaze with magical fire.

Turn to page 42.

Black Canary brings her borrowed warhorse to a stop as the Circe monster stomps toward her. The horse rears in terror, so she leaps off its back and lets it flee. She stands alone as the enormous Circe-Harpy looms over her.

"Look at you, little bird," Circe laughs.

"Look at you, big target," Canary replies.

POWWW!

Supergirl hits the Circe-Harpy from behind.

"Circe packed a punch, but so do I," Supergirl says.

The sorceress staggers but doesn't go down. "Urgh, you tricked me," she growls as she digs her talons into the ground to keep standing.

"Let's see if I can deliver a knockout blow," Black Canary says.

She unleashes the full sonic power of her Canary Cry at point-blank range. Even Supergirl covers her ears.

EEEEEEEEEE!

The Circe-Harpy tumbles head over talons as she's thrown back by the sonic blast. When she finally stops rolling, Circe decides she has had enough. She wobbles up into the sky and flies away from the fight.

Supergirl starts to chase after the Harpy monster, but Black Canary stops her.

"Let Circe go for now. We have another problem," Canary says. "We have to stop the Beastiamorphs from destroying the homes of the horse riders."

"That's right!" Supergirl says. "The Flash is still running a tornado through the group of wagon homes."

"And Green Arrow is attacking the warriors who are defending them," Black Canary says. "We have to stop our friends."

"What are we waiting for?" Supergirl asks. She pulls Black Canary under her arm and flies toward the battle.

Turn to page 45.

Wonder Woman pulls herself up the length of the golden rope as the transformed Superman speeds through the sky. When she's close enough, she flips onto the Beastiamorph's back. She loops the rest of the lasso around his torso.

"Listen to me!" Wonder Woman commands.

The magical Lasso of Truth glows with power. Superman stops struggling.

"Good," Wonder Woman says. "Now, you will answer my questions."

Superman droops his rhino head. Wonder Woman lets out a sigh of relief. The Beastiamorph is obeying her. That means the lasso can break through Circe's spell.

"Who are you?" Wonder Woman asks.

"I am Kal-el of Krypton," Superman replies. "I am Clark Kent of Earth. I am Superman!"

Superman has come back to his normal mind. But his Beastiamorph body stays the same. He looks at his rhino arms and legs.

"What happened?" Superman asks.

"Circe," Wonder Woman answers as she gets off his back and hovers in the air. "She turned the male Justice League members into Beastiamorphs. She wants to use them to take over this planet. You and Cyborg were attacking a mountain fortress."

"I can't believe I was helping her," Superman says. "But I'm OK now. You can release me."

Wonder Woman knows that the Lasso of Truth won't let him tell a lie. She lets her teammate go.

Suddenly Superman takes off at super-speed! Wonder Woman follows him back to the fortress. When she lands, the transformed hero is already holding a giant block of stone above his head. The warriors start to swarm around him.

"Oh no!" Wonder Woman gasps. "Is he about to finish the job he started?"

She's worried that Circe's spell has taken control of him again. She twirls her golden lasso, ready for anything.

Turn the page.

To Wonder Woman's surprise, Superman tosses the block back onto the wrecked fortress wall. He uses his heat-vision to melt it in place.

"I've come to fix what I broke," Superman says to the warriors. "I'm sorry."

The people cheer and start to help with repairs.

Wonder Woman lands next to Superman. "A heads-up would've been nice. You had me worried," she tells him. "But if things are under control here, I have to find Big Barda. Last I saw, she was battling Cyborg. Where could they be?"

CRAAAASH!

Barda and Cyborg fly out of the nearby forest and smash into the fortress wall.

"Oh. There they are," Wonder Woman says.

She twirls her Lasso of Truth and wraps it around Cyborg's bear-like chest. Soon he's helping Superman rebuild the fortress too.

Big Barda grins. "That's what I call teamwork!"

THE END

To follow another path, turn to page 11.

"OK, Circe is pretty tough," Huntress admits. She runs toward the sorceress and fires her crossbow as fast as she can reload.

Circe transforms the bolts before they can reach her. She turns them into harmless worms and centipedes that drop to the ground. Huntress pulls smoke bombs from her Utility Belt and throws them at Circe.

BWHAAAM! FWHOOOSH!

Circe disappears behind a hazy cloud. Huntress can't see Circe, but Circe can't see the hero either.

"Now would be a good time for phase two!" Huntress shouts.

Power Girl hovers above the battle and hears Huntress with her super-hearing. Using her X-ray vision, she spots Circe through the smoke.

"Here it comes, you wicked witch," Power Girl says and drops the enchanted robot house she's been holding.

THWUUUUMP! The house lands on Circe.

The impact shakes the deck. The villagers and the Beastiamorphs pause in the middle of battle to look over. They see a house lying upside down with its enchanted legs sticking straight in the air.

"It worked!" Huntress exclaims as Power Girl lands on the town ship.

"You sound surprised," Power Girl says.

"I told you it was risky," Huntress replies.

The super heroes walk closer to the house. They see Circe's legs poking out from under it.

"Yep, it's just like in that old movie, *The Wizard of Oz*!" Power Girl says.

Suddenly the home's enchanted legs disappear. A shout comes from across the deck. The villagers watch in surprise as the Beastiamorphs transform back to humans.

Batman and Aquaman rush over to their teammates. They stare at Circe's legs.

"Don't worry," Huntress tells them. "Circe is knocked out for now. But she'll be mad when she wakes up."

Turn the page.

Power Girl uses her super-strength to lift the house. Huntress, Batman, and Aquaman start to grab Circe, but the villagers block them.

"We will punish this criminal according to our own laws," one of the people declares.

Batman nods. "It's your right," he says.

The Justice League heroes step aside. The villagers lift Circe, carry her to the edge of the town ship, and toss her overboard.

SPLASH!

Then the villagers go back to their business.

"I guess that's the punishment. I'll go get Circe so we can lock her away," Aquaman says. "She'll be really mad if she wakes up defeated *and* wet."

As he dives into the water, Power Girl turns to her friends. "Then we'll round up the rest of our teammates and figure out a way home," she says. "This adventure isn't over yet."

THE END

To follow another path, turn to page 11.

Supergirl and Black Canary arrive in the middle of chaos.

Families flee as their empty wagon homes whirl up and around in a tornado created by The Flash in his Beastiamorph form. The hero's head, arms, and legs look like a cheetah's. His limbs move at blurring speed. In the sky near the tornado, Green Arrow flaps his huge hawk wings. He fires smoke arrows and grenade arrows at the horse warriors.

"I can get The Flash while you handle Green Arrow," Black Canary tells Supergirl. "Now drop me onto a warhorse, and let's save these people!"

Supergirl spots a stray horse and plops Black Canary into the saddle. The heroes charge into action.

Canary rides through a rain of trick arrows that Green Arrow is shooting down at the horse warriors. She carefully aims her Canary Cry and destroys the arrows before they reach the riders. She continues toward the tornado.

"*EEEEEE!*" Canary shouts at The Flash.

Turn to page 47.

The sonic blast crashes into The Flash, and the transformed hero gets knocked out. The tornado falls apart. The wagons land with a heavy *THUMP!*

Up in the sky, Supergirl faces Green Arrow in his hawk form. He shoots a grenade arrow, but it bursts harmlessly against her. Then Supergirl launches her own attack.

FWOOOOSH!

She blows a gust of super-breath at the Beastiamorph. It sends him spinning. Supergirl catches him before he hits the ground.

Green Arrow is so dizzy that he passes out. Supergirl stands over him as Black Canary rides up. The Flash is draped across the saddle.

"Well, we've defeated two Beastiamorphs," Supergirl says. "But we can't change them back, and we can't get home without Zatanna."

"We can use the comm units in our belts to call her. If she's on the planet, she'll find us and we can regroup," Black Canary says as she gets off her horse. "We'll figure something out."

Turn the page.

Suddenly a huge mass of warriors surrounds the super heroes. The leader jumps down from her horse and marches over to Black Canary.

"You are heroes," the leader declares. She gives Canary a huge hug. "We will celebrate!"

The warriors cheer and toss their helmets into the air. Supergirl and Black Canary are surprised to see that they're all women.

"Join us!" the leader says.

"Um, OK," Black Canary replies.

The crowd cheers again. Supergirl shoots her teammate a questioning look.

"What?" Black Canary whispers. "We might be here for a while waiting for Zatanna. And it wouldn't be polite to refuse such a nice invitation."

THE END

To follow another path, turn to page 11.

"Let's stay together," Wonder Woman decides. "We'll defeat them in no time!"

The super heroes charge the Beastiamorphs. Wonder Woman tackles Superman before he can crash into the fortress wall. They tumble away.

Meanwhile Cyborg aims the sonic cannon on his arm. His human half may be bear-like, but his mechanical half is as powerful as ever. He fires at Big Barda and a group of warriors.

THWOOOOM!

The warriors tumble back, but Barda pushes through the mighty sound wave. She warps her arms around Cyborg's furry chest and powers up her Aero-Discs. They both fly across the battlefield, and together they hit the fortress wall.

"Grrrr!" the Beastiamorph growls. Face to face with Barda, Cyborg's mechanical eye glows red.

ZZZZT! A beam strikes out at Barda's head. She dodges it just in time.

CLAAAANG! Barda head-butts him in reply. Her helmet connects with Cyborg's metal skull.

Turn the page.

"Uhhh . . . ," Cyborg moans.

The Beastiamorph is dazed, but not for long. He uses his bear-like strength to break free from Big Barda's hold. He fires his boot jets and rises into the air.

"I won't let you escape," Barda declares. She energizes her Mega-Rod and leaps up.

BWHAAAAAM!

Big Barda strikes her transformed friend, and he goes flying out of sight.

Barda gulps. "Oops."

She's about to go help Wonder Woman when Cyborg zooms back. He's mad. He bares his sharp teeth and aims all his weapons.

"That doesn't scare me!" Barda shouts. "I was once a Female Fury of Apokolips. I threw off the control of Darkseid, the most dangerous foe in the universe. I'm not afraid of your puny weapons!"

Cyborg launches his attack. A flurry of missiles, lasers, energy beams, and sonic blasts head straight toward the super hero.

THWOOOM! BWOOOOMF! CRAAASH!

The weapons strike Big Barda all at the same time. She's knocked back into the wall of the fortress, and it collapses. Blazing explosions and clouds of smoke and dust cover the area.

When the air clears, a pile of debris is all that's left of the wall. Barda is buried under it. Cyborg lands next to the mound and roars in triumph.

The native warriors stand nearby, watching everything. The strange woman warrior fought the bear creature to help them. Now she has fallen. A battle cry goes up. Avenge her!

The warriors charge toward Cyborg. He snarls and aims his sound cannon. Suddenly the giant pile of rubble explodes outward!

"Like I said, puny weapons," Barda says as she leaps out from the debris and arches through the air.

WHAAAAM! She lands feet-first on the Beastiamorph. The impact drives him into the ground.

Turn to page 58.

STOMP! STOMP!

The rest of the enchanted houses plod toward the villagers near the tower.

"Let's split up. You take care of those houses. I'll deal with Circe and the Beastiamorphs. Somehow," Huntress decides.

Power Girl zooms at the robot houses as Huntress runs toward the tower. She scans the houses with her X-ray vision to check if anyone is inside. When she's sure they're empty, she activates her heat-vision.

ZZZZZRRRRRT!

The beams slice through the buildings' legs. The houses fall onto the deck and stay there.

"Well, that was quick," Power Girl says. She turns back to join Huntress.

POOF! A cloud of smoke suddenly appears. Zatanna steps out of the swirling puff.

"Sorry we're late!" she says.

"We?" Power Girl asks.

"I brought Etrigan. He loves a good fight," Zatanna replies and points to the demon. He's already shooting mystical fire at Circe.

"Good. We need help protecting that central tower," Power Girl tells her teammate. "We think it controls the whole fleet."

Zatanna looks up at the tall structure. "I think it does more than that," she says. "I sense powerful magic inside. I'm going to take a look."

Power Girl launches toward the battle as Zatanna walks across the deck. When she reaches the fighting, she utters a backward-spoken spell.

"*Em dnuora mrof noitcetorp fo erehps,*" Zatanna says. A spell of protection surrounds her.

Nearby, Huntress grapples with Batman in his bat-like form. They tumble toward Zatanna. She doesn't flinch. The Beastiamorph and Huntress bounce off her spell.

BWOOONG!

The blow stuns Batman. Huntress quickly pins back his wings to keep him from attacking.

Turn the page.

As Zatanna continues forward, Beastiamorph Aquaman spots her and snaps his shark teeth. He rushes toward her with his trident raised, but Power Girl blocks it with her invulnerable body.

BWAAAANG!

She grabs the tip of the weapon and shakes it at super-speed. Aquaman holds on and is shook as if gripping a super-fast jackhammer.

Circe also sees Zatanna heading for the tower. But the sorceress can't do anything about it. She dodges another blast of fire. Etrigan is keeping her busy. The demon's magic is almost as powerful as hers!

It makes Circe even more furious. Her anger makes her reckless.

"Eat this!" Circe shouts and unleashes a massive stream of energy at Etrigan.

She expects it to vaporize the annoying creature, but he opens his mouth and gulps it down. He feeds on the power.

"Yum! Yum! Yum!" Etrigan says with a smile.

Turn to page 62.

Black Canary jumps off her horse. Then she blasts Circe with an ear-splitting Canary Cry. The sonic wave shreds the feathers off the Harpy's body. Suddenly Circe looks like a plucked chicken!

"Oops!" Canary giggles.

Enraged, Circe transforms into a different beast from Greek myth. She grows scales and sprouts nine serpent heads. The heads snap their jaws at Black Canary, but she uses her acrobatic skills to leap out of the way.

"From Harpy to a Hydra. That's not much of an improvement," Canary says.

Suddenly the heads turn toward Supergirl, who is lying unconscious on the ground nearby. She's an easy target for Circe's wrath.

"Hey! Pick on someone who can defend herself!" Black Canary shouts.

Circe-Hydra doesn't care. She picks Supergirl up in her jaws and tries to crush her.

CRAAAACK!

But Circe's serpent fangs shatter!

Turn the page.

Circe shakes her Hydra head in surprise and spits Supergirl out of her mouth.

"It's like chomping on solid steel, isn't it?" Canary asks. "Your teeth can't do any damage— her body is invulnerable."

"Yours isn't," Circe says. She shrieks at Black Canary with all nine heads.

The force of the sound knocks Canary off her feet. She rolls across the ground.

"I have the power of the legendary Sirens at my command!" Circe-Hydra boasts. "Their voices lured men to their doom!"

"Too bad you're off-key," Black Canary replies. "Let me give you an example of perfect pitch."

Canary directs a tremendous Canary Cry at Circe-Hydra. Circe returns the attack. The two blast each other with sonic fury.

The earth under their feet starts to shake. It splits and cracks. Huge pits open up around Circe and Black Canary. Supergirl, who is lying nearby, tumbles into one of the gaps.

"No! Supergirl!" Black Canary yells.

She immediately breaks off her attack and runs to the edge of the pit. She looks down and sees her teammate resting on a ledge not far below. She's safe—for now. But Canary wonders what sort of magic Circe used on Supergirl to keep her unconscious for so long.

THUMP! THUMP!

Black Canary hears the Circe-Hydra lumbering up from behind. She also hears the monster panting for breath. It sounds like a runner gasping after a hard sprint.

"You might have volume, but you don't have any vocal endurance," Black Canary says as she turns to face the creature. She fills her lungs with air, ready to blast Circe.

Before Black Canary can unleash her Canary Cry, one of Circe-Hydra's serpent heads strikes out like a rattlesnake.

It grabs the hero in its jaws!

Turn to page 65.

"Rhaaaar!" Cyborg growls through sharp animal teeth. He squirms under Big Barda's feet.

"Give up, Cyborg," Barda says. "Let me get you home. We will bring you back to your human self."

"Grrraaarr!" the bear-like hero roars. Then he fires his boot jets and blasts off.

"OK, we'll do it the hard way," Barda says. She powers up her Aero-Discs and flies after him.

They don't travel far. Cyborg heads to where the transformed Superman is fighting Wonder Woman.

"Cyborg is looking for backup," Barda realizes. She smiles. "This could be a magnificent battle."

Big Barda pushes her Aero-Discs to full speed.

WHAAAAM!

She slams into Cyborg. They both topple into Superman, shoving him away from Wonder Woman. The tangled trio falls toward the only part of the fortress wall that's still standing.

"Barda! Look out!" Wonder Woman shouts.

CRAAASH!

The warning comes too late. The wall crumbles onto Wonder Woman's friends—and starts to fall onto the people defending the fortress. The Amazon Princess leaps over and gets under the wall. She holds it up so the warriors can escape.

"Barda! Where are you?" Wonder Woman shouts, looking around. "Are you all right?"

BWHAAAAM!

Big Barda smashes up out of the rubble. Cyborg and Superman follow right after her. She has a big grin on her face.

"I'm fine! I can't say the same for these guys!" Barda replies.

She grabs a metal statue from the rubble and twists it around the Beastiamorphs.

"That's not going to hold them for long!" Wonder Woman says as she drops the piece of fortress wall.

"It doesn't have to," Barda replies. She grips her crackling Mega-Rod and swings.

Turn the page.

Barda fires her Mega-Rod against the twisted metal. The rod's energy flows through it and zaps the Beastiamorphs, knocking them out cold.

The native warriors surround the rhino and bear creatures. They grumble angrily.

"They sound mad," Barda says. "We must go after Circe, but first we better get our friends back to the Watchtower."

"How? Zatanna's spell brought us here," Wonder Woman says.

Barda pulls a small box from her belt. She presses a button on it. **BOOM!** The warriors step back as a glowing tunnel suddenly appears.

"It's a Boom Tube. Never leave home without one," Barda explains. "It'll let us travel instantly."

Big Barda picks up the Beastiamorphs and steps into the Boom Tube. Wonder Woman follows.

"I like making a dramatic exit," Barda says as the tunnel closes. **BOOM!**

THE END

To follow another path, turn to page 11.

Etrigan grows gigantic from the magic power. He swings a huge fist at Circe and knocks her far out to sea. Then he lets out a loud burp and shrinks down to normal size.

The people of the town ship cheer. Etrigan takes a bow. But the battle isn't over yet.

Batman opens his leathery wings wide and breaks loose from Huntress. Aquaman rams Power Girl with his shark head.

The fighting starts up again, so no one notices that Zatanna has reached the tower. She puts her hands on it. She feels magical power inside, and something else. Some*one* else.

"Who are you?" Zatanna whispers. "Let me in."

Say the magic word, a voice says. It isn't speaking out loud. It's speaking inside Zatanna's mind.

"Please," Zatanna replies.

Zatanna blinks and suddenly she's inside the tower. She's surprised to see the long, serpent-like neck of a golden sea creature. But she isn't afraid. She feels calm as she floats to the top of the tower.

There, Zatanna sees the head of the beautiful beast. She can't help herself. She reaches out.

As soon as she touches it, the sea being's mind connects with Zatanna's. The hero instantly sees the history of the sea fleet! It makes Zatanna more determined to save the people from Circe.

The sea being feels Zatanna's thoughts. *Who is Circe?* it asks.

Zatanna remembers her battles with the sorceress. The sea being sees and feels each one.

BLAAAAM!

Suddenly the walls of the tower explode outward. Circe hovers nearby in the air.

"I knew something valuable was inside this tower," the sorceress says, looking at the golden sea creature.

"Circe," Zatanna growls. It's the hero's voice, but it's the sea being speaking through her. "You dare to attack my people."

"*Your* people? Who do you think you are?" Circe says. She still thinks it's Zatanna talking.

Turn the page.

"I am the Goddess of the Sea. I carry this ship upon my back as the fleet travels the oceans," the being replies. "You will not harm them."

ZAA-POWWW!

Golden energy strikes out from the sea goddess through Zatanna. Circe is blasted down onto the deck. She does not get up.

Zatanna is released from the connection. She floats slowly to the deck. She lands next to Power Girl and Huntress as Aquaman and Batman return to their human forms.

"Thank you for your help," Zatanna says to the goddess and bows low. Then she tells her friends, "Let's go home."

With a backward-spoken spell, Zatanna brings the Justice League members from around the planet to the ship. All the Beastiamorphs are back in human form. The Justice League teammates take Circe into custody and surround Zatanna.

"Emoh su tropelet," she says.

THE END

To follow another path, turn to page 11.

Fortunately the Hydra head that snatches Black Canary is the one with the shattered teeth. Canary is unharmed, but the Hydra's jaws press hard against her torso. She can't take a deep breath for a strong Canary Cry.

The serpent neck slowly twists around so that Black Canary faces Circe-Hydra's central head.

"I'm going to crush you like a twig, little bird," Circe vows.

"Didn't your mother ever teach you not to talk with your mouth full? Such bad manners," Black Canary says. "And talk about bad breath. Phew!"

"I don't have bad breath!" Circe replies. She starts to get angry.

"What was that? You're mumbling. I could teach you some exercises to help with that," Black Canary continues. "Just give me an 'ah' in C-minor. Oh, that's right, you're off-key."

"I will grind you between my teeth!" Circe snarls. She lifts Black Canary toward her wide jaws.

Turn the page.

The mouth holding Black Canary opens as it starts to drop her into the monster's main maw. The pressure lets up on Canary's torso, and she can fill her lungs at last.

She looks down the dark throat of the Hydra and smells its rotten serpent breath. Black Canary almost gags. But she's at point-blank range and must not waste this chance.

EEEEEEEEEEEEEEEEEEEEEE!

The Circe-Hydra shudders at the intense impact. All her serpent heads whip around wildly. Black Canary is tossed into the air. She hits the ground at the same time as the Circe-Hydra. Neither of them gets up.

A few moments later Circe returns to her human form. Off in the distance, so do the Beastiamorphs. The Flash and Green Arrow race to the side of their fallen teammate. Green Arrow kneels beside Black Canary and holds her gently in his arms.

"She's hardly breathing!" Green Arrow says. "What happened?"

"She defeated the evil conqueror! Praise to the fallen champion!" the leader of the horse riders says as she gallops up. The warriors all remove their helmets in respect.

"It's true," Supergirl adds as she rises shakily from the nearby pit. "She saved us all."

There is a moment of silence.

"Hey . . . I'm not dead. I was . . . just resting," Canary says weakly as she opens her eyes.

Green Arrow hugs her so hard that he almost squeezes the breath out of her lungs again. The horse warriors cheer.

"So what do we do with Circe?" Green Arrow growls. The sorceress still lies unconscious on the ground.

One of the horse warriors uses her boot to shove Circe into the pit.

"Works for me," Black Canary says.

THE END

To follow another path, turn to page 11.

Wonder Woman sees Big Barda pause. "Go! I can handle these two," the Amazon says as she dodges the horn on Superman's rhino head. "You need to find Circe so she can turn our friends back to humans."

Barda nods. "Right. Good luck."

She looks down at the Mother Box in her hand. The small cube makes a clear **PING!** sound as it turns on.

"Mother Box, find Circe and bring me to her location," Barda tells the device.

The Mother Box pings again in response. Then it instantly creates a Boom Tube.

BOOM!

The interdimensional tunnel of glowing energy appears with a sound like thunder.

But as Barda steps into the tunnel, she sees the Beastiamorphs charging toward her. They're wrapped up together in Wonder Woman's golden lasso, and they're dragging the hero behind them!

Turn to page 70.

Big Barda dodges the Beastiamorphs. They hurtle right into the Boom Tube. Wonder Woman is pulled along with them.

"I guess we're going to find Circe together!" Wonder Woman says before she disappears into the tunnel.

Barda runs after her friends. The tunnel closes with a **_BOOM!_** It opens at their destination with another loud **_BOOM!_**

Wonder Woman and the Beastiamorphs are the first to arrive. Superman and Cyborg gallop out of the Boom Tube like a team of runaway horses. Even though Wonder Woman knows she can use her golden Lasso of Truth to command the Beastiamorphs, she doesn't try to stop them.

Because they're heading straight for Circe.

Wonder Woman sees the sorceress hovering above a grassy meadow. She's blasting bolts of magical energy at an army of horseback warriors.

"This must be another one of the three empires Circe wants to conquer," Wonder Woman realizes.

BOOM!

Behind her, Wonder Woman hears the Boom Tube close. It means that Barda has arrived. But the Amazon's attention is on Circe.

Wonder Woman knows she has to stop Circe's attack on the people. She grips the Lasso of Truth.

"Fly to Circe!" she commands.

Superman launches into the air. Cyborg fires his boot jets. Wonder Woman leaps onto their backs and rides them like a surfboard.

"You horse warriors are no match for my magic," Circe says as she attacks them from above. "I'll be the ruler of this world in no time—huh?"

Circe stares at the outrageous sight of Wonder Woman riding over on the backs of two super-powered Beastiamorphs. Her surprise gives Wonder Woman the chance to act. The hero releases the Beastiamorphs from her lasso and wraps it around Circe instead.

Circe struggles against the golden lasso. She's shocked that it has the power to hold her.

Turn to page 76.

Power Girl can think of only one action. She swoops down at tremendous speed and stomps on the Circe monster with both feet.

WHAAAAM!

The creature releases its grip and falls off the side of the town ship. The Circe monster flails in the water. Even though it looks like a giant crab, it can't swim. It starts to sink.

"Don't tell me I have to rescue Circe from her monstrous mistake," Power Girl groans.

Before Power Girl can move, Circe solves the problem herself. She returns to human form and flies out of the water.

"Well, that didn't work," the sorceress says. "But I know a classic spell that might do the trick."

She aims a bolt of magic at a villager on the deck. **POOF!** The person is transformed into a mythical griffin Beastiamorph! It flaps its huge eagle wings and takes to the air. Then it roars like a lion and heads straight at Power Girl.

Meanwhile on the deck below, everything is in chaos. As soon as the Circe monster's weight was gone, the ship sprang back up. Now the vessel rocks violently back and forth as it tries to right itself.

Batman flaps his giant wings and escapes into the air. Aquaman jams his trident into the deck and steadies himself with it. Huntress feels a little seasick.

Huntress stays on her feet by shooting a grapnel rope and anchoring it to the side of the tower. She quickly works her way hand over hand and moves toward the tower's base.

But the Beastiamorphs aren't going to let her journey be an easy one. Batman swoops overhead and throws Bat-grenades from his Utility Belt. His aim isn't very good as a Beastiamorph, but Huntress is still pounded by the blasts.

Then she sees Aquaman stalking toward her. Dozens of villagers cling to the shark beast, trying to stop him. Nothing slows him down.

Turn to page 79.

Zatanna steps back. Etrigan doesn't need help. He has Circe all wrapped up. Besides, she needs to focus on using her magic to wake Black Canary.

But before Zatanna can do anything, the ball of fire explodes. The blast sends Zatanna and Etrigan tumbling across the meadow. In the sky, Supergirl protects Canary from the fiery burst.

Circe stands, unharmed. Her outfit is smoldering a little. So is her temper. Her eyes blaze with mystical fire.

"Uh-oh," Etrigan says.

"*Mrof noitcetorp fo dleihs!*" Zatanna says and casts a backward-spoken spell of protection.

Circe unleashes a searing fountain of fire at Zatanna and Etrigan. It hits Zatanna's magical shield like molten lava. Both heroes can feel the heat. Etrigan holds Zatanna's hand and pours his demon power through her and into her shield spell. Circe's fire can't break through.

"You're going to need more than that," Etrigan tells Circe.

The sorceress grins. "I'm just getting started."

Circe's whole body starts to glow. Suddenly an eruption of magical energy blasts out.

BWAAAAAM!

It throws Supergirl and Black Canary far through the air. The horse riders are knocked down like bowling pins. The wave hits The Flash's tornado and shreds it. Even Green Arrow is smacked to the ground.

When the brilliant light of the magical explosion fades, giant chasms stretch across the meadow. Circe stands on a pillar of rock in the center of the destruction. She looks around at the result of her blast. She doesn't see Zatanna or Etrigan.

"Ha! It looks like I got rid of that meddling magician and her pet demon," Circe says. "Good riddance. Now I can conquer this planet in peace."

Turn to page 83.

The Beastiamorphs see that their master is in trouble. They're no longer bound by the lasso, so they rush to attack Wonder Woman.

POWWW!

Big Barda comes from behind and strikes them with her Mega-Rod. They hit the ground, knocked out cold. The horseback warriors cheer.

"Stand guard over the beasts, but don't hurt them," Barda tells the warriors.

Barda goes over to where Wonder Woman and Circe have landed. The sorceress is wrapped up in the golden lasso like a squirming mummy.

"By the power of the Lasso of Truth, I order you to turn the Beastiamorphs back to human form," Wonder Woman says.

"I . . . will . . . not," Circe replies. It takes all her strength to fight the lasso's power.

"I can make her talk," Big Barda growls and puts her face next to Circe's.

Up close, Circe sees something fierce in Barda's eyes. It makes her gulp.

POOF! Suddenly a puff of white smoke appears. When it clears, Zatanna and Etrigan stand nearby.

"Surprise!" Etrigan chuckles.

"Ah, I see that Merlin's little pet demon has arrived," Circe says from the ground.

Etrigan's skin erupts with furious demon fire, but Zatanna holds up a hand. "Ignore her," she says calmly. "Thanks to Wonder Woman's lasso, my spell will work on Circe much easier now. *Mrof namuh ot shpromaitsaeB eht erotser, ecriC!*"

Zatanna's backward-spoken spell makes Circe grimace. But she still fights against it.

"OK, maybe not that easy," Zatanna admits. "Etrigan, you and I must hold the lasso. Our combined magic should overcome Circe."

Etrigan and Zatanna grip the rope. Etrigan pours his fiery magic through the Lasso of Truth. Zatanna repeats her spell. Wonder Woman commands Circe to obey Zatanna.

Circe and the lasso blaze with light.

Turn the page.

"Noooo!" Circe shouts—just before she surrenders to the magical attack.

A wave of spell power bursts outward from the sorceress. It hits the two Beastiamorphs. A second later they transform from rhino and bear back into their human forms. The native warriors gasp in awe as Superman and Cyborg fly to their teammates' side.

"What happened?" Superman asks. He looks around. "Where are we?"

"We'll tell you when we get everyone back to the Watchtower," Zatanna promises. "But first . . . *Lamina na otni ecriC nrut!*"

The golden lasso wrapped around the villain glows brilliantly, and she starts to change shape. Circe turns into a fluffy rabbit! Zatanna puts the rabbit into her top hat.

"Now we can go home," Zatanna says.

THE END

To follow another path, turn to page 11.

Huntress braces herself to battle both Beastiamorphs on her own. She can hear the roars of some sort of monster in the sky above. The sounds seem to be getting closer—fast.

Huntress risks a glance upward. She sees Power Girl and a giant griffin plunging down toward the tower.

"Uh-oh," Huntress says.

The griffin and Power Girl smash into the tower. Huntress uses her acrobatic skills to roll away from the griffin as it tumbles off the town ship. Aquaman is knocked off his feet. Finally.

A violent rumble travels through the entire town ship. Suddenly giant tentacles burst up through the tower.

"What is *that*?" Huntress gasps.

"Kuthulu!" the villagers shout as they run away from the tower.

"That doesn't sound good," says Huntress.

Turn to page 81.

The tentacles whip around wildly. Power Girl barely escapes their grasp. She blasts them with her heat-vision, but it has no effect.

On the deck, Huntress watches the tentacles brace themselves on the deck like a tripod. They lift the rest of the enormous creature out from the tower.

The monster has the slimy body of a snail, but it's a thousand times bigger. It has hundreds of spines that drip thick goo.

"Ugh!" Huntress groans. "And I thought Circe's crab creature was nasty."

The monster strikes out at everything and everyone with its giant tentacles. It smashes houses. It knocks people overboard. Power Girl pounds the creature with super-punches, but she can't stop its rampage.

"It's going to destroy the ship!" Power Girl says.

"Nothing is going to stop me from conquering this fleet!" Circe yells as she swoops out of the sky. "Not the Justice League or some ugly monster!"

Turn the page.

Circe grows until she's twice the size of the monster. She grabs the creature with one giant hand and hurls it far out to sea. The monster sinks below the waves and doesn't come up.

The villagers cheer Circe as she returns to her normal size. The super heroes look on in surprise.

"They're calling me their liberator!" Circe says with a laugh. "It seems the monster was an evil dictator who had taken over the fleet. He was forcing them to defend him in the tower."

"The people think Circe is a hero," Power Girl whispers to her teammate. "We can't fight her now."

"You've won this one, Circe," Huntress says. "Release the Beastiamorphs, and we'll leave."

"Fine. I don't need them anymore. And the sooner you heroes are gone, the sooner I can start ruling my new empire," Circe says. **POOF!** She teleports the Justice League back to Earth. "Now, should I call myself empress, queen, or goddess?"

THE END

To follow another path, turn to page 11.

Circe's thoughts of victory don't last long.

POOF! Zatanna and Etrigan appear out of thin air right in front of the evil sorceress.

POWWWW!

Etrigan punches Circe with his thick fist. The powerful blow stuns the villain, and she stumbles backward into the deep pit in the ground.

"I *really* love surprises," Etrigan says.

"I'm just glad we teleported away before Circe created that explosion," Zatanna says. She looks around at the damaged land and toppled wagon homes. "We'll have to help these horse warriors with repairs."

"But first, where are Supergirl and Black Canary?" Etrigan wonders. "The blast must've really sent them flying. I don't see them anywhere."

"I'll find them with a spell," Zatanna says.

But before she can speak the words, the ground shakes. It crumbles out from under their feet!

Turn the page.

Another gigantic creature of clay rises from the ground. But this is Zatanna's creation. It combines the powers of her Justice League teammates. It has the wings of Hawkgirl and the claws of Vixen.

"Erutaerc s'ecriC kcatta!" Zatanna orders.

Her creation flaps its wings and flies at Circe's monster before it reaches the wagons. The creation's sharp claws dig into the golem and hold it tight. Etrigan sends a stream of demon fire at the trapped golem, burning it completely.

Circe stares at the pile of ash. "This is too much trouble," she mutters and teleports away.

"She'll never be a cosmic conqueror with that attitude," Etrigan says.

"It's not over yet. Circe still has to reverse her Beastiamorphs spell," Zatanna says. "Let's find Supergirl and Canary and continue the fight."

Etrigan nods. "Circe might have given up, but we have not!"

THE END

To follow another path, turn to page 11.

Big Barda watches the Beastiamorphs get ready to attack again. She puts the small Mother Box device back in her belt.

"I cannot leave you to face them by yourself," she tells Wonder Woman. "I'll stay."

Big Barda and Wonder Woman get ready to take on their transformed friends. Suddenly a shout rises up from the warriors defending the fortress. They are gathered behind the super heroes and wave their swords and spears.

"I think we've just become their leaders," Barda realizes. "We've chased off the sorceress and defeated her Beastiamorphs. Well, almost."

"We can't put the people in harm's way. We're here to *protect* them," Wonder Woman says.

"Um, too late," Barda replies.

The warriors charge past them and toward the Beastiamorphs. Superman zooms across the battlefield, ready to ram the warriors with his rhino horn. Cyborg lets out a bear-like roar and powers up his sonic cannon.

Turn the page.

"We've got to keep them apart!" Wonder Woman shouts.

"Don't worry," Barda says. "I have an idea."

Big Barda powers up her Aero-Discs. They lift her into the air and above the battlefield. She aims her Mega-Rod and fires an energy blast.

BAWHOOOOM!

Down on the ground, Wonder Woman feels the earth shift under her feet like a wave as Barda's blast makes impact. She struggles to stay upright while the warriors around her tumble and fall. But they quickly get back on their feet and are ready to attack. So is Wonder Woman. So are the Beastiamorphs.

But the ground between them is split open. Barda created a pit to keep the Beastiamorphs away from the people of the planet.

The warriors shout in frustration. They want to fight the rhino and bear creatures!

"Sorry," Big Barda tells the people. "But this is not your fight."

Turn to page 96.

Power Girl decides to use her heat-vision to break the creature's grip on the town ship. She aims the hot beams at one of the hard claws.

ZZZZZRRRRRT!

The Circe monster howls in pain but doesn't let go. Instead, she swipes at Power Girl with her other claw.

WHAAAAM!

The claw catches the hero and knocks her far out to sea.

Circe is furious now. So she transforms into an even larger sea monster—a kraken! She wraps her squid-like tentacles around the town ship. She starts to pull the vessel underwater.

"Circe's gone mad. She's going to destroy the ship!" Huntress shouts.

Water rushes through the village, and the huge town ship sinks beneath the waves. Aquaman easily swims over to the Circe-Kraken. Batman flaps into the air. The villagers struggle to stay above water.

Turn the page.

As Huntress treads water, she worries about the villagers. How can she save everyone? But then their clothing inflates!

"I guess if you live on the ocean, you have outfits that float," Huntress says in relief. Then she sees a shark fin circling her.

"Uh-oh. Aquaman," Huntress realizes.

She quickly loads her mini crossbow and fires a bolt to chase him off. But suddenly the ocean waves start to toss and churn. The Beastiamorph swims away, and Huntress watches as the whole town ship rises out of the water and into the air.

At the very bottom of the ship is Power Girl. She's returned and uses her super-strength to lift it to safety. The villagers in the water cheer. Circe-Kraken roars with rage.

The monster leaps from the ocean and tries to grab the ship. Power Girl flies higher and carries the vessel out of Circe's reach. The Circe-Kraken shrieks one more time, and then sinks below the surface. Aquaman follows her into the depths.

Power Girl uses her X-ray vision to search for the Circe-Kraken, or whatever form of underwater monster the sorceress might have changed into. But Circe is gone. So is Beastiamorph Aquaman. Power Girl lowers the town ship back onto the surface of the ocean at last.

The rest of the fleet comes to help the people still in the water. Hundreds of boats rush to the rescue. Power Girl plucks villagers out of the sea at super-speed and puts them back onboard. Suddenly her super-hearing picks up a familiar voice.

"I could use a little help here," it says. "Bad bat! Bad bat!"

Power Girl looks around with her super-vision and spots Huntress treading water. But she's also fighting off Beastiamorph Batman at the same time. He hovers above the water and swats his powerful wings at her.

"Oops!" Power Girl exclaims and zooms to help her teammate.

Turn to page 99.

"I took the energy from the fireball and used it to create this creature. Thanks!" Circe says.

At Circe's command, the dragon blasts flames at the Justice League teammates. They dodge the attack, but it sets the meadow grasses on fire. Supergirl flies off to blow out the blaze with her super-breath. Zatanna, Etrigan, and Black Canary face Circe and the dragon.

"Three against two doesn't seem fair. Beastiamorphs come to me!" Circe says. Green Arrow flies over on his hawk-like wings. The Flash pumps his cheetah legs and races to Circe's side. "There. Now it's four against three."

"You call that fair?" Black Canary asks.

"I call it winning," Circe replies. "Beastiamorphs, attack! Dragon, blast them!"

As the creature takes a deep breath, Black Canary fills her lungs too and prepares to unleash a Canary Cry. Etrigan gets ready to fight the Beastiamorphs.

Zatanna whispers a backward spell. But it's not directed at the attackers.

"STOP!" a voice suddenly yells.

Everyone is so surprised by the order that they actually halt. The Beastiamorphs, heroes, and sorceress watch as a single horse warrior wearing full native armor and a helmet gallops over to them.

"Who *are* you people?" the warrior shouts angrily. "You're destroying our pastures and family wagons. You're frightening our herds. Take your fight somewhere else!"

Circe stares down at the rider. She's amused and impressed by the warrior's bravery.

"And who are *you*?" Circe asks.

"I am the queen of the Kiron Horse Tribes," the warrior replies. She takes off her helmet. A woman's blue-skinned face is revealed.

"You look like an Amazon. I hate Amazons," Circe says.

The dragon inhales a huge breath, ready to burn the warrior queen.

Turn to page 103.

The warriors can only watch as Wonder Woman leaps across the huge gap. Big Barda swoops out of the sky. The Beastiamorphs charge forward at the heroes, growling and roaring.

"Ugh! These guys are all brute strength," Wonder Woman says as Superman shoves her with his rhino head.

"All brawn and no brains," Barda agrees as she swats away Cyborg's bear paw. She delivers a punch. **POWWW!**

"Which means we can outsmart them," Wonder Woman says as she flips her foe onto his back. **THWAAAM!**

"Do you have a plan?" Barda asks.

CLAAANG!

"We set a trap," Wonder Woman replies.

WHAAACK!

"With what?" Barda asks.

SMAAACK!

"A Boom Tube," Wonder Woman says.

Barda grins. "I like it. But how do we trick them into something as obvious as a Boom Tube? It's hard to miss a huge, glowing energy tunnel."

"We don't make it obvious," Wonder Woman replies. "Just follow me and get ready to activate the Boom Tube with your Mother Box."

Wonder Woman bursts into action against Superman. Using her Amazon speed, she delivers quick blows with her feet and fists. Superman's rhino brain reacts slowly, but it reacts furiously.

"Rhaaaar!" the Beastiamorph roars.

"Follow meeee!" Wonder Woman shouts as she jumps into the pit Barda created. Superman leaps after his foe.

"Let's join the party, Cyborg," Barda says.

She swings her powerful Mega-Rod and knocks the half bear, half machine hero into the hole. Then she jumps down after him.

As the native warriors gather around the edge of the pit, they suddenly hear a loud sound.

BOOM!

Turn the page.

Wonder Woman and Big Barda roll out of the Boom Tube. Superman and Cyborg follow behind. But before the Beastiamorphs can react, the super heroes leap back into the transport tube. **BOOM!** It disappears.

Superman and Cyborg look around at their new surroundings. They're no longer on the planet. They're in a large metal holding cell!

BOOM! The Boom Tube opens again. Wonder Woman and Barda walk out into the Justice League meeting room on the Watchtower.

"Using yourself as bait to trick Superman into the pit was brilliant," Big Barda says. "The small space was perfect for trapping the Beastiamorphs into a Boom Tube."

"At least they're safe in the Watchtower holding cells. Now, let's get back to that planet. We'll find Circe and make her return them to human form," Wonder Woman declares.

BOOM!

THE END

To follow another path, turn to page 11.

Power Girl scoops up Huntress and then
knocks the Beastiamorph into the sea. Batman
can't swim in his animal form. He flails his wings
and starts to sink.

"I've got you," Power Girl says with a sigh.
She pulls Batman from the water. He's so tired he
doesn't fight back.

As Power Girl flies toward the town ship, she
sees magical energy swirling all over the vessel.
She and her teammates quickly land on the deck.

"Did Circe come back?" Power Girl asks.

"No, it's Zatanna," Huntress says. She points
over to the Justice League magician, who's
standing by some destroyed houses.

"Sorry I teleported here late and missed all
the action," Zatanna says. Her spells repair the
buildings. "I'm just undoing what Circe did."

"And I'll do it again!" Circe's voice booms.

The sorceress rises from the ocean. She's in
human form, but she's blazing with magical fury.
She lands and marches toward the central tower.

Turn the page.

A door suddenly opens at the base of the tower. A handsome man walks out. Circe stops in her tracks at the sight of him.

"Odysseus?" Circe whispers. "Can it be you? My one and only love? You sailed away so long ago. I thought I'd never see you again."

"I am the captain of this vessel, and this fleet!" the man says. "I don't know who this Odysseus fellow is, but he is a fool to leave someone as beautiful as you."

"What a bunch of—" Huntress starts to say, but Zatanna stops her with a look.

"Shhh! Just watch," Zatanna whispers.

"You have the face of my dear Odysseus, and for that I will spare this fleet. But only if you come back to my island with me—and stay," Circe says.

"I agree to your terms," the captain replies. "I will sacrifice myself for my people. And what a delightful sacrifice it is!"

POOF! Circe teleports them from the ship.

Turn to page 102.

"That was . . . noble?" Huntress says.

"That was Etrigan disguised as Odysseus," Zatanna reveals. "I brought him here and then used an illusion spell to hide his demon form."

Suddenly Beastiamorph Batman transforms into a human. A few moments later, Aquaman leaps out of the water and joins his teammates on deck. He's back to his normal self too.

"What happened? The last thing I remember was being on the Watchtower," Aquaman says.

"Circe happened," Batman growls.

"She must've released her Beastiamorph spell," Zatanna says. "'Odysseus' must be doing a good job of distracting her."

"Circe will be furious when she finds out she's been tricked," Power Girl says.

"We'll be ready for her. In the meantime, let's get the rest of our teammates and go home," Zatanna says. She speaks a backward spell.

POOF!

THE END

To follow another path, turn to page 11.

The queen of the Kiron doesn't back off. She quickly raises a metal shield to block the fiery attack. Circe's eyes widen in shock at the sight of the image decorating it.

"That looks like Medusa! Where did you get that shield?" Circe demands.

"It is the Royal Shield. The goddess gave it to me," the queen says, but she does not lower the shield.

"W-which goddess?" Circe asks nervously.

Zatanna steps forward. "If I remember my Greek mythology, Perseus cut off the enchanted head of Medusa and gave it to Athena," she says.

The queen nods. "Yes!" she says. "The goddess is named Athena! She protects the horse tribes."

"Athena is also a goddess of Olympus. She's more powerful than you, Circe. She might get mad if you attack people under her protection," Zatanna points out. "Do you really want to challenge her?"

Turn the page.

"Well, I don't see Athena protecting the horse riders right now," Circe growls.

"I can summon her," the queen says and starts a chant.

"Not if you never finish!" Circe declares. She commands the dragon, "Burn her!"

The dragon unleashes its fiery breath. The queen holds up the Medusa shield, and it blocks the flames. The warrior continues speaking her spell.

After releasing a huge surge of fire, the dragon runs out of breath. The queen finishes the chant.

The ground under their feet shakes. Clouds in the sky darken. Lightning crackles. The two Beastiamorphs huddle near their master. Circe looks worried.

"Hmph! If Athena wants this crummy little planet, she can have it," Circe says.

The sorceress teleports away. *POOF!*

The dragon falls apart in a shower of sparks as soon as Circe disappears. The Beastiamorphs return to human form. The heroes look very confused.

"Where are we?" The Flash wonders.

"What happened?" Green Arrow asks.

"Just a neat trick, as Supergirl put it," Zatanna says. She waves her arms and speaks a backward spell. The storm clouds break up. The warrior queen disappears like mist.

"Illusions!" Etrigan realizes with a hearty laugh. "Zatanna bluffed Circe and chased her off with *illusions*!"

"Remind me never to play cards with Zatanna," Green Arrow says.

THE END

To follow another path, turn to page 11.

AUTHOR

Laurie S. Sutton has read comics since she was a kid. She grew up to become an editor for Marvel, DC Comics, Starblaze, and Tekno Comics. She has written Adam Strange for DC, Star Trek: Voyager for Marvel, plus Star Trek: Deep Space Nine and Witch Hunter for Malibu Comics. There are long boxes of comics in her closet where there should be clothing and shoes. Laurie has lived all over the world, and currently resides in Florida.

ILLUSTRATOR

Erik Doescher is a concept artist for Gearbox Software and a professional illustrator. He attended the School of Visual Arts in New York City and has freelanced for DC Comics for almost twenty years, in addition to many other licensed properties. He lives in Texas with his wife, five kids, two cats, and two fish.

GLOSSARY

conquer (KONG-kuhr)—to take control of a place or people by fighting

deck (DEK)—the upper, outside floor on a ship that goes from one end of the vessel to the other

fleet (FLEET)—a group of ships under one command

golem (GOH-luhm)—a clay figure from Hebrew folklore that's been brought to life by magic

Harpy (HAHR-pee)—a monster from Greek mythology that is half woman and half bird

Hydra (HI-druh)—a serpent from Greek mythology with nine heads; when one head is cut off, two more grow in its place

illusion (i-LOO-zhuhn)—something that appears to be real but isn't

invulnerable (in-VUHL-ner-uh-buhl)—impossible to injure

kraken (KRAH-kuhn)—a gigantic sea monster from Norwegian myths

sonic (SON-ik)—having to do with sound waves

sorceress (SAWR-ser-is)—a woman with magical powers

teleport (TEL-uh-pawrt)—to move from one place to another instantly

transform (trans-FORM)—to change something completely

unconscious (uhn-KON-shuhss)—not awake; being unconscious is often the result of an injury or drug

CIRCE

Real Name:
Circe

Occupation:
Sorceress

Base:
Island of Aeaea

Height:
5 feet 11 inches

Weight:
145 pounds

Eyes:
Blue

Hair:
Purple

Circe is an immortal sorceress from ancient Greece who has a flair for the dramatic. She's spent a great deal of time plotting against Wonder Woman, because she believes it's the Amazon Princess' fault she hasn't become all-powerful. Circe practices the art of dark magic, and her mystical abilities make her a dangerous foe. She can control minds, fire energy blasts, create illusions, teleport instantly, and transform objects and people. Over the years, Circe has tricked many people into doing her bidding. One never knows where she might pop up next.

- Circe loves nothing more than humiliating others. Her favorite attack is to change opponents into ugly animal-creatures called Beastiamorphs. She then uses the transformed people to cause chaos and carry out her commands.

- The sorceress spends the majority of her time on the island of Aeaea. Circe uses a special plant that grows there to make an elixir called vitae. This elixir allows Circe to stay eternally youthful and beautiful.

- One of Circe's most ambitious schemes was causing a war between gods around the world. She tricked the almighty beings into cosmic combat in an effort to destroy the goddess Gaea. It took all the mighty powers of Wonder Woman and the heroes of Earth to put an end to the villain's evil plot.